Drone

W9-DHN-659

The Honeybee Colony

THREE KINDS OF HONEYBEES live together as a colony in the beehive. First, each colony has one queen bee whose only job is to lay eggs. Each hive also has a small number of male bees called drones, whose only job is to mate with the queen bee. All the other bees in the hive — tens of thousands of them — are female worker bees, like Beatrice. A young worker bee's first job is cleaning honeycomb cells. As she ages, she performs other tasks — caring for the young, producing wax and building honeycomb, unloading and storing nectar and pollen collected by older bees, guarding the hive and, finally, foraging for nectar and pollen.

Pollen

FLOWER POLLEN is another important food for honeybees. The pollen grains are gathered from flowers and carried in special receptacles on the bee's hind legs, called pollen baskets. When a bee has a full load, she carries the pollen back to her hive, where her sisters unload it, and pack it away in the comb. As a bee collects pollen, she also performs an important service for the flowers she visits. Pollen grains that stick to her body are transferred from one flower to another, pollinating them. This pollination is necessary for the flower to reproduce.

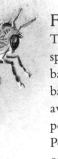

Ouch!

A HONEYBEE'S SOLE MEANS OF DEFENSE is its sting. A honeybee can sting a human being only once, and then the honeybee dies. For this reason a honeybee will usually sting a human being only if the hive is threatened in some way.

Hive, Sweet Hive

HONEY is made by honeybees and is their primary source of nourishment. Honeybees live and store their honey in beehives. Although people have harvested honey from wild honeybees since prehistoric times, long ago we learned that bees could be persuaded to store honey in hives provided for them by beekeepers. The shape of these manmade hives has varied from place to place and over time, but the main idea has always been the same — to provide a place for bees to live and store honey so that the honey can be easily harvested by the beekeeper.

Honeycomb

HONEYBEES store honey in honeycomb they build inside the hive. Honeycomb is made up of many six-sided cells built out of wax produced by the worker bees. Its design makes the honeycomb extremely strong and allows the bees to store the maximum amount of honey using the minimum amount of beeswax.

Bea's Own Good

Written by **Linda Talley**

Illustrated by **Andra Chase**

MarshMedia, Kansas City, Missouri

32424104939115

To sisters around the world who help each other.

Text © 1997 by Marsh Film Enterprises, Inc.

Illustrations © 1997 by Marsh Film Enterprises, Inc.

First Printing 1997
Second Printing 2000
Third Printing 2004

Published by

A Division of Marsh Film Enterprises, Inc.
P. O. Box 8082
Shawnee Mission, KS 66208

Library of Congress Cataloging-in-Publication Data
Talley, Linda.
    Bea's own good/written by Linda Talley; illustrated by Andra Chase.
        p. cm.
    Summary: A young French honeybee learns the rules to keep the honeycomb strong, to make the best honey, and to keep the bees safe. Endpapers feature factual information about bees, the Château of Villandry, and France.
    ISBN 1-55942-092-8
    [1. Bees—Fiction. 2. France—Fiction.] I. Chase, Andra, ill. II. Title.
PZ7.T156355Be 1997   96-44328
[E]—dc21

Book layout and typography by Cirrus Design

Special thanks to John Chase, Carol Talley, and Miss Margaret Farnsworth Marsh — who has already met her own Bea.

Printed in Hong Kong

$\mathcal{I}$ arrived in this world with the French springtime, but for the first fourteen days of my life, I did not leave the beehive that is my home.

As a result, I did not know that spring had arrived in the bee-master's garden, that the wisteria was in bloom on the garden wall and buttercups, anemones and sweet violets in the meadow beyond. There were many other things I didn't know then, *mon ami*.

One thing I learned very quickly is that there are many rules a young honeybee must follow if she is to make her way safely and happily in the world.

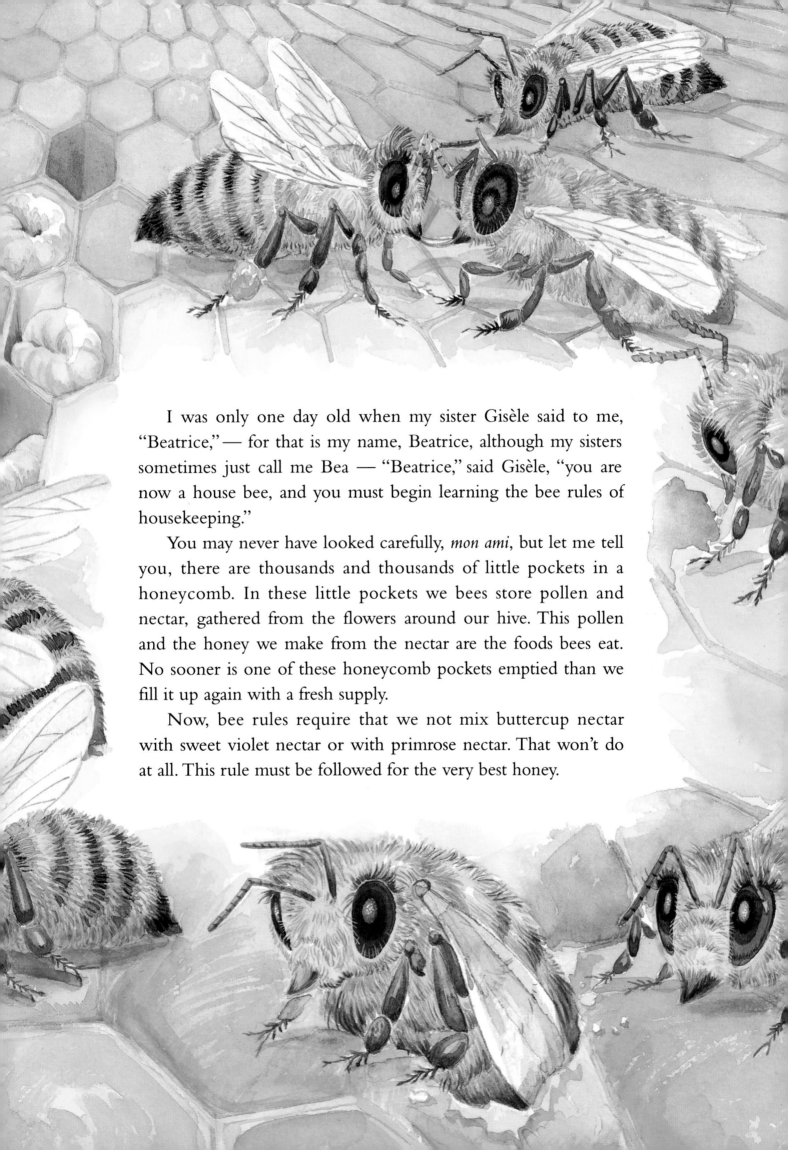

I was only one day old when my sister Gisèle said to me, "Beatrice," — for that is my name, Beatrice, although my sisters sometimes just call me Bea — "Beatrice," said Gisèle, "you are now a house bee, and you must begin learning the bee rules of housekeeping."

You may never have looked carefully, *mon ami*, but let me tell you, there are thousands and thousands of little pockets in a honeycomb. In these little pockets we bees store pollen and nectar, gathered from the flowers around our hive. This pollen and the honey we make from the nectar are the foods bees eat. No sooner is one of these honeycomb pockets emptied than we fill it up again with a fresh supply.

Now, bee rules require that we not mix buttercup nectar with sweet violet nectar or with primrose nectar. That won't do at all. This rule must be followed for the very best honey.

Furthermore, each of the little honeycomb pockets must be cleaned *just so*, according to bee rules, so that the honey doesn't spoil. No litter can be left clinging to the sides. Oh, no. No crumbs of beeswax can be left in the bottom. No, not one.

Also, when it comes time to build new pockets in the honeycomb, they can't have four sides or five sides or eight sides, but each and every pocket must have exactly six sides. My sister Céleste explained to me that this makes our honeycomb strong so that it can hold many pounds of honey.

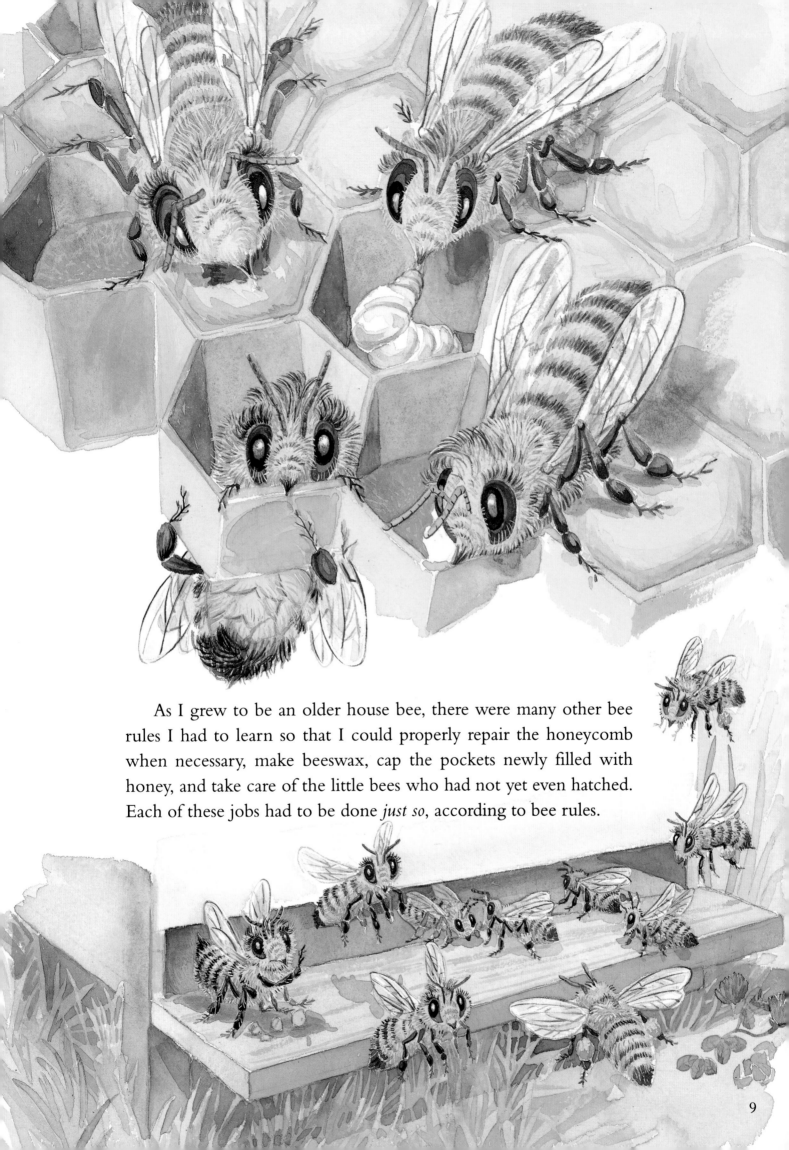

As I grew to be an older house bee, there were many other bee rules I had to learn so that I could properly repair the honeycomb when necessary, make beeswax, cap the pockets newly filled with honey, and take care of the little bees who had not yet even hatched. Each of these jobs had to be done *just so*, according to bee rules.

9

Some days I grew very tired of doing everything *just so*. I longed for the day I would become a field bee, with no rules to follow. Then I could leave the hive each morning in search of nectar. What a life!

In fact, when I was about two weeks old, I was allowed to take short training flights outside the hive at midday. Sometimes I would venture inside the walls of the bee-master's garden, and on very warm days I would see him with his wife and daughter eating lunch on the terrace.

I was surprised one day to see a pretty little pot of honey on the lunch table. I managed to fly down to get a taste before Madame shooed me away. That is the day I learned that we share our honey with the bee-master.

Another day, as I hovered in the air over the bee-master's table, I overheard something amazing. An expedition was planned. The next morning, Cati, the bee-master's daughter, would be visiting a very special place. "It is the most beautiful garden in the world," sighed the bee-master.

I could not believe he had said such a thing. Surely, there could be no garden more beautiful than the bee-master's garden. You see, *mon ami*, I had never traveled more than a few feet from my own hive and there were many things I did not know.

On that very night, my sister Sylvie said to me, "Rest well tonight, little sister, for tomorrow you must go to the meadow to collect pollen." I decided that moment that I would go with the bee-master's daughter on her expedition. "But you must not go far," said Sylvie sternly, as though reading my mind. "In the early spring a honeybee must not fly far from the hive. That is one of the most important bee rules. A cold wind could blow in. Then you would be a very chilly bee and unable to fly back home."

"I am a field bee now," I thought to myself. "I can make my own rules. The bee-master is letting his daughter go to the beautiful garden. If it is not against the rules for her, surely a little bee can safely follow."

The next morning, I sat in the sunshine at the entrance to our hive, waiting impatiently for Cati. At last she came out the door with her mother.

"It's a pretty morning," said the bee-master's wife, "but the weather is changeable this time of year. You must take a sweater and scarf." With that, Cati jumped on her bicycle and pedaled down the road. Humming to myself, I flew after her.

The sky was the deepest blue. Wildflowers bounced in the spring breeze. White cows happily soaked up the sun. "This is the life," I thought to myself. "No more cleaning up beeswax crumbs, no more feeding babies, no more doing everything *just so!* No more bee rules!"

We passed through the village. It was market day and — wonder of wonders — there stood the bee-master behind a little stand with many jars of golden honey! On we went. Cati fairly flew down the road and I buzzed happily above her.

I flew and I flew and when I thought I could fly no further, we came over the crest of a hill. Suddenly, there it was before us.

The most beautiful garden in the world!

But this was more than a garden, *mon ami*. It was a wonderland filled with flowers laid out like an enormous tapestry. Not only were there flowers, but ponds and fountains and swans and walkways wide enough to drive a carriage through. And towering over it all was a beautiful château.

I flew from flower to flower, humming to myself. I collected pollen until I could carry no more.

I had settled on a wisteria blossom to rest a moment, when I felt a chilly wind stir my wings.

I had been so busy, I had not noticed the heavy gray clouds that now completely covered the sun. I was suddenly very cold. Cati was cold too and had pulled on her sweater and tied her scarf around her head.

Together we started our long trip home. But as I flew, the air about me grew colder. I grew stiffer and stiffer, and my wings grew heavier and heavier. I knew I could not fly much further and wished with all my heart that I had saved my visit to the most beautiful garden in the world for a summer day.

Now I knew why it was against bee rules to go to the garden today, even though it was all right for the bee-master's daughter to go. People have sweaters to put on if they get cold. Bees do not. And when the clouds roll in on a day in early spring, a girl's legs do not hang from her like lead weights the way my wings hung uselessly at my sides that day.

Finally I could go no further, and I fell from the sky.

When I awoke, I found myself in the bottom of Cati's bicycle basket. I crawled to the top to see what I could see. I was back in the bee-master's garden, and there was my hive only a few feet away! Even so, I was so cold that I could not fly to the hive.

Suddenly there was the bee-master himself looking down on me. "I will help you, my little friend," he said.

He gently picked me up and carried me to the hive entrance.
In I went.

I was immediately surrounded by my sisters.

"Bea!" cried Gisèle. "We have been so worried!"

"It is too cold this afternoon for a bee to be out," scolded Céleste.

"Where have you been?" asked Sylvie."

"I have been to the most beautiful garden in the world," I told them. "But I should not have gone so far. If not for good luck and the kindness of the bee-master, I would never have made it back to my home."

"Well, now you know what bee rules are for!" said Sylvie.

And that, *mon ami*, is how I learned that bee rules are for Bea's own good!

Dear Parents and Educators:

Rules help define our responsibilities to one another and the parameters of acceptable behavior in our homes and communities. Children need the direction rules provide for their personal safety and development. They need the security of knowing that they are not yet totally responsible for their daily lives. Following rules helps youngsters develop patience, understanding, and sensitivity to the needs of others. In time an awareness of the importance of rules will help children take reasonable calculated risks. Their self-confidence will soar as they use these lessons to develop positive relationships within the family and the community.

Bea's story helps children explore how rules and limits relate to the responsibilities and privileges of growing up. Children will feel Bea's frustration with having to follow so many rules. It is not always fun to control one's behavior, but children will learn from Bea that their choices have consequences and that the rules of home and school are made for their "own good."

To help youngsters better understand the message of *Bea's Own Good*, discuss the following questions with them:

- What rules did Bea have to follow when she was a house bee? Did these rules have a purpose?

- Why did Bea's sister tell her not to go far from the hive?

- Why did Bea decide to break this rule?

- What are some rules you follow at home? At school?

- Have you ever broken a rule?

- What did you learn?

Here are some ideas to help families develop and enforce necessary limits and regulations:

- Too many rules can overwhelm children. Identify the most important issues for your family.

- Allow children a voice in developing family rules. Sharing control on YOUR terms means children will feel less need to try to take control on THEIR terms.

- Within reason, let natural consequences teach children to respect rules and limits.

- When a rule is broken, focus on how your child will deal with the consequences of his or her behavior.

- Assure children with your words and actions that you love them even when a rule is broken.

- Remember — pushing the limits is a normal part of growing up. Your children are developing independence.

- Children learn most effectively from adult example. Share some of the rules you follow and discuss their importance.

Available from MarshMedia

These storybooks, each hardcover with dustjacket and full-color illustrations throughout, are available at bookstores, or you may order at www.marshmedia.com or by calling toll free: 1-800-821-3303.

Aloha Potter! Written by Linda Talley, illustrated by Andra Chase. 32 pages. ISBN 1-55942-200-9.

Amazing Mallika, written by Jami Parkison, illustrated by Itoko Maeno. 32 pages. ISBN 1-55942-087-1.

Bailey's Birthday, written by Elizabeth Happy, illustrated by Andra Chase. 32 pages. ISBN 1-55942-059-6.

Bastet, written by Linda Talley, illustrated by Itoko Maeno. 32 pages. ISBN 1-55942-161-4.

Bea's Own Good, written by Linda Talley, illustrated by Andra Chase. 32 pages. ISBN 1-55942-092-8.

Clarissa, written by Carol Talley, illustrated by Itoko Maeno. 32 pages. ISBN 1-55942-014-6.

Dream Catchers, written by Lisa Suhay, illustrated by Louis S. Glanzman. 40 pages. ISBN 1-55942-181-9.

Emily Breaks Free, written by Linda Talley, illustrated by Andra Chase. 32 pages. ISBN 1-55942-155-X.

Feathers at Las Flores, written by Linda Talley, illustrated by Andra Chase. 32 pages. ISBN 1-55942-162-2.

Following Isabella, written by Linda Talley, illustrated by Andra Chase. 32 pages. ISBN 1-55942-163-0.

Gumbo Goes Downtown, written by Carol Talley, illustrated by Itoko Maeno. 32 pages. ISBN 1-55942-042-1.

Hana's Year, written by Carol Talley, illustrated by Itoko Maeno. 32 pages. ISBN 1-55942-034-0.

Inger's Promise, written by Jami Parkison, illustrated by Andra Chase. 32 pages. ISBN 1-55942-080-4.

Jackson's Plan, written by Linda Talley, illustrated by Andra Chase. 32 pages. ISBN 1-55942-104-5.

Jomo and Mata, written by Alyssa Chase, illustrated by Andra Chase. 32 pages. ISBN 1-55942-051-0.

Kiki and the Cuckoo, written by Elizabeth Happy, illustrated by Andra Chase. 32 pages. ISBN 1-55942-038-3.

Kylie's Concert, written by Patty Sheehan, illustrated by Itoko Maeno. 32 pages. ISBN 1-55942-046-4.

Kylie's Song, written by Patty Sheehan, illustrated by Itoko Maeno. 32 pages. (Paper Posie, LLC) ISBN 0-911655-19-0.

Ludmila's Way, written by Linda Talley, illustrated by Andra Chase. 32 pages. ISBN 1-55942-190-8.

Minou, written by Mindy Bingham, illustrated by Itoko Maeno. 64 pages. (Paper Posie, LLC) ISBN 0-911655-36-0.

Molly's Magic, written by Penelope Colville Paine, illustrated by Itoko Maeno. 32 pages. ISBN 1-55942-068-5.

My Way Sally, written by Mindy Bingham and Penelope Paine, illustrated by Itoko Maeno. 48 pages. (Paper Posie, LLC) ISBN 0-911655-27-1.

Papa Piccolo, written by Carol Talley, illustrated by Itoko Maeno. 32 pages. ISBN 1-55942-028-6.

Pequeña the Burro, written by Jami Parkison, illustrated by Itoko Maeno. 32 pages. ISBN 1-55942-055-3.

Plato's Journey, written by Linda Talley, illustrated by Itoko Maeno. 32 pages. ISBN 1-55942-100-2.

Tessa on Her Own, written by Alyssa Chase, illustrated by Itoko Maeno. 32 pages. ISBN 1-55942-064-2.

Thank You, Meiling, written by Linda Talley, illustrated by Itoko Maeno, 32 pages. ISBN 1-55942-118-5.

Time for Horatio, written by Penelope Paine, illustrated by Itoko Maeno. 48 pages. (Paper Posie, LLC) ISBN 0-9707944-7-9.

Toad in Town, written by Linda Talley, illustrated by Itoko Maeno. 32 pages. ISBN 1-55942-165-7.

Tonia the Tree, written by Sandy Stryker, illustrated by Itoko Maeno. 32 pages. (Paper Posie, LLC) ISBN 0-911655-16-6.

Companion videos and activity guides, as well as multimedia kits for classroom use, are also available. MarshMedia has been publishing high-quality, award-winning learning materials for children since 1969. To order or to receive a free catalog, call 1-800-821-3303, or visit us at www.marshmedia.com.

France

FRANCE is the largest country in Western Europe. Its capital is Paris, considered by many people the most beautiful city in the world. French people have made great contributions to the world's culture and learning, particularly in the fields of architecture, literature, painting, music and philosophy. The varied geography of France includes flat plains and wheat fields in the north central region, ski resorts in the French Alps, and palm trees and beaches on the sunny Riviera.

The Loire River Valley

BEATRICE AND HER SISTERS live in the Loire River Valley of France. The Loire River is France's longest river. Along its banks are many beautiful châteaux, or castles, built by French royalty and nobility. Many are open to the public.

The Gardens of Villandry

THE CHÂTEAU OF VILLANDRY, which Bea visits with Cati, was completed in 1536. Its fame rests on its terraced gardens. On one level, colorful vegetables are grown in geometrical patterns, accented with fruit trees, rose bushes and vine-covered arbors. On a second level, flowers and shrubs are laid out in equally complex designs. On the highest terrace a water garden is built around an ornate lake in the shape of an antique mirror.

To Market

MOST FRENCH TOWNS have a weekly open-air market where shoppers may buy fresh produce, bread, cheese, sausages and other meats, new and used clothing, live rabbits and fowl, household items, tools and knives, furniture, plants and flowers. At almost every village market one will find a beekeeper selling honey, beeswax, and honey candy.

From Nectar to Honey

HONEY is made from nectar that bees collect from flower blossoms. The nectar is carried back to the beehive and packed into the honeycomb cells. The bees add substances to the nectar that prevent mold and bacteria from forming, and they fan the nectar with their wings to evaporate most of the water in the nectar. When enough water is removed, *voila*, we have honey! The beekeeper harvests part of the honey, but he must leave enough for the bees to eat.